Dear Parent:

Your child's love of reading starts here!

Every child learns to read in a different way and at his or her own speed. Some go back and forth between reading levels and read favorite books again and again. Others read through each level in order. You can help your young reader improve and become more confident by encouraging his or her own interests and abilities. From books your child reads with you to the first books he or she reads alone, there are I Can Read Books for every stage of reading:

SHARED READING
Basic language, word repetition, and whimsical illustrations, ideal for sharing with your emergent reader

BEGINNING READING
Short sentences, familiar words, and simple concepts for children eager to read on their own

READING WITH HELP
Engaging stories, longer sentences, and language play for developing readers

READING ALONE
Complex plots, challenging vocabulary, and high-interest topics for the independent reader

I Can Read Books have introduced children to the joy of reading since 1957. Featuring award-winning authors and illustrators and a fabulous cast of beloved characters, I Can Read Books set the standard for beginning readers.

A lifetime of discovery begins with the magical words "I Can Read!"

*Visit www.icanread.com for information
on enriching your child's reading experience.*

Pete the Kitty and the Unicorn's Missing Colors
Text copyright © 2020 by Kimberly and James Dean
Illustrations copyright © 2020 by James Dean
Pete the Kitty © 2015 by Pete the Cat, LLC
Pete the Kitty is a registered trademark of Pete the Cat, LLC, Registration Number 5576697
All rights reserved. Printed in the United States of America.
No part of this book may be used or reproduced in any manner whatsoever without written permission
except in the case of brief quotations embodied in critical articles and reviews. For information address
HarperCollins Children's Books, a division of HarperCollins Publishers, 195 Broadway, New York, NY 10007.
www.icanread.com

Library of Congress Control Number: 2020931598
ISBN 978-0-06-286846-6 (trade bdg.) —ISBN 978-0-06-286845-9 (pbk.)

Book design by Chrisila Maida
22   CWM   13
❖
First Edition

My First SHARED READING

I Can Read!

Pete the Kitty
AND THE UNICORN'S MISSING COLORS

by Kimberly & James Dean

HARPER
An Imprint of HarperCollinsPublishers

Pete sees his friend
Stevie the unicorn
at the playground.

Stevie looks sad.

"Hi, Stevie," says Pete.

"What's wrong?"

"The magic unicorn dance
party is tonight," says Stevie.
"But I lost all the colors
in my rainbow tail."

"I can help!" says Pete.
"We can use
my magic paintbrush!"

"Where did you last see
your colors?" Pete asks.

"Um," Stevie says.
"When I was playing
in the park."

9

The park is very big.
Stevie looks worried.

"We'll never find my colors
before the dance party,"
Stevie says.

"Which colors are you
missing?" asks Pete.

"Red, orange, yellow, green,
blue, and purple are gone,"
Stevie says.

"Look!" Pete points
his magic brush
at a berry patch.
"Let's borrow some red!"

Pop! A magic red blaze
appears in Stevie's tail.
"Wow!" says Stevie.

"Now we know what to do,"
says Pete.

"Great!" says Stevie.

"Do green next!"

"Green is everywhere!"
says Pete.
"The grass is green.
The trees are green."

Pop! Stevie's tail gets
a green blaze.
Stevie prances.

"That butterfly is yellow!"
says Pete.
Pop! Stevie's tail gets
a yellow blaze.

"Hurry, Pete!" says Stevie.
"Three more colors to go!"

"This flower is orange!"
says Pete.
Pop! Stevie's tail gets
an orange blaze.

"Keep going, Pete,"
Stevie says.
"The party starts soon."

"The lake is blue!" Pete says.
Pop! Stevie's tail gets
a blue blaze.

"One more left," says Stevie.

"The clouds are purple!"
shouts Pete.

Pop! Stevie's tail gets
a purple blaze.
"Yay!" Pete and Stevie cheer.

Stevie jumps for joy.
Pete found all the
missing colors!

"I love my rainbow tail!"
says Stevie.
"Come with me to the party!"

Stevie and Pete dance at the
magic unicorn dance party.

Stevie's rainbow tail
is a big hit!

"Thanks, Pete!" says Stevie.
"It's cool to help friends,"
says Pete.